COMIC CHAPTER BOOKS

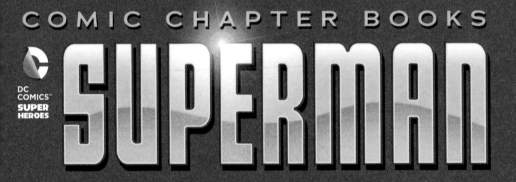

DC COMICS™
SUPER HEROES

STONE ARCH BOOKS
a capstone imprint

Superman: Comic Chapter Books are published by
Stone Arch Books,
A Capstone Imprint
1710 Roe Crest Drive
North Mankato, Minnesota 56003
www.capstoneyoungreaders.com

Star33543

Library of Congress Cataloging-in-Publication Data is
available on the Library of Congress website.

ISBN: 978-1-4342-9133-2 (library binding)

ISBN: 978-1-4342-9137-0 (paperback)

ISBN: 978-1-4965-0095-3 (eBook)

Summary: The super-villain known as Brainiac loves
nothing more than adding new data about civilizations
to his memory banks--and then destroying those
civilizations so the data is more valuable. He has
long coveted Metropolis and has sought to take it for
himself, but the Man of Steel has always been able
to repel the robotic villain. But this time, Brainiac has
found a sentient ship that collects entire worlds...and
led it directly to Earth! Can Superman stop two world-
stealing intelligences at the same time?

Printed in the United States of America in Stevens Point, Wisconsin.
032014   008092WZF14

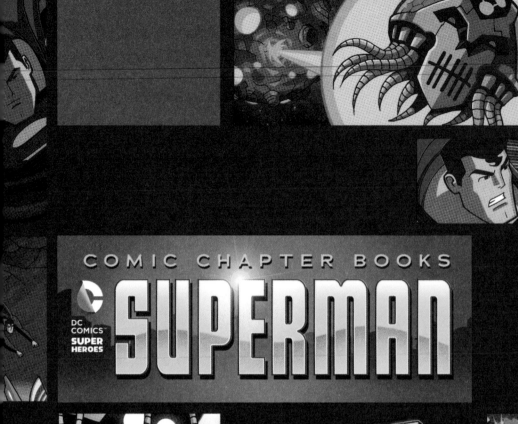

COMIC CHAPTER BOOKS

DC COMICS SUPER HEROES

SUPERMAN

THE PLANET COLLECTOR

written by
Laurie S. Sutton

illustrated by
Luciano Vecchio

Superman created by Jerry Siegel and Joe Shuster
By special arrangement with the Jerry Siegel family

TABLE OF CONTENTS

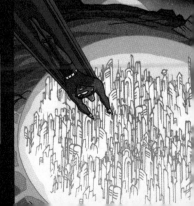

CHAPTER 1

ALIEN ENCOUNTERS

Brainiac was on the hunt. His skull-shaped spaceship zipped through a dying quadrant of deep space. The suns here were burning out and fading into cinders. The planets that revolved around those stars were sliding into permanent darkness. Entire civilizations were perishing.

Which was exactly what Brainiac wanted.

He was a collector of worlds. A harvester of knowledge and technologies. His mission was to seek out advanced cultures and insert them into his database . . . and that usually meant watching them die.

Once a planet's knowledge was absorbed, that world was destroyed. That made Brainiac's data unique — and therefore much more valuable.

Brainiac's current quest had brought him to this particular doomed sector of space. The cultures here would soon be gone. Their knowledge would be lost. Several rich sources of information would cease to exist. It would be like they never existed at all.

That is, unless Brainiac harvested the planet's data.

BLIP!

A blinking on the ship's sensors drew his attention. Brainiac was an android and thus was linked to his spacecraft by data tendrils connected to the ports on his skull. He guided the ship by thought, as if part of his own body.

BLIP!

The sensor blinked again. Something was out there. And it was getting closer.

"Display," Brainiac ordered. The image of a planet flashed before Brainiac's eyes.

Brainiac saw a world turning to ice, starved of light from its faint, dying sun. Yet there was heat rising from its frozen surface. Little clusters of warmth dotted the globe.

"Scan wavelengths," Brainiac said.

The sensors revealed that the heat was artificial, meaning it did not come from volcanoes or forest fires. Rather, it came from cities. There were beings on the planet struggling to survive. And they had the technology to do it.

Brainiac decided to investigate. He turned his skull-ship toward the planet, hungry to discover if there was anything new he could add to his database.

As he approached the planet, Brainiac was startled by an unexpected sight. Another spaceship was in orbit above the frozen surface!

It wasn't often that Brainiac was surprised. His memory banks contained images of many incredible things. Over the years, during his journeys through space, he had seen things that mere mortals could never experience.

But this alien ship surprised Brainiac. It was not like anything he had encountered before. It resembled a giant asteroid. Most of its surface was covered with chunks of space debris.

Slowly, Brainiac flew his skull-ship closer to the object. He saw towers of bright metal clustered in circles that supported engine pods. That was the only clue Brainiac had that this was a ship and not a hunk of space junk.

"Impressive," Brainiac admitted as he looked at the strange vessel. It was gigantic. "Perhaps it has technology I can acquire."

He commanded the skull-ship to take a course closer to the immense craft. The nearer Brainiac got to the ship, the better he could see its surface.

It was as rough and irregular in shape as an asteroid. In fact, to the untrained human eye, it would look exactly like a chunk of harmless space rock.

"What is the purpose of such a design? Stealth? Camouflage?" Brainiac wondered. "How intriguing. I must learn more. Hold position and scan."

ZWOOOOP!

ZWOOOOP!

ZWOOOOP!

Sensors swept over the megaship. Once more, Brainiac was surprised.

FZZZZZRT!

A force field suddenly surrounded Brainiac's ship. The alien leviathan seemed to be attempting to take control of Brainiac's skull-shaped vessel.

THE MEGASHIP PULLS BRAINAC'S SHIP INSIDE...

HOW UNEXPECTED. MY SENSORS HAVE TRIGGERED A TRACTOR BEAM. I HAVE NO CONTROL.

...AS WELL AS AN ALIEN CITY!

UNEXPECTED.

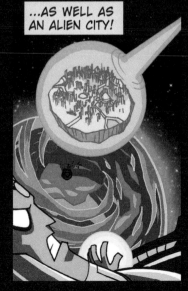

"All conventional efforts to escape have failed," he said. "I must devise new strategies. Calculating . . ."

* * *

Meanwhile, thousands of light years away, across the entire galaxy, another battle for survival was being fought. The bright blue globe known as Earth was being invaded!

A rain of fluffy space spores drifted down on the city of Metropolis. While they were in the air, the spores looked harmless. They floated on the breeze like dandelion puffs.

At first, the people thought they were pretty. But then the spores made contact with the ground and the buildings, and they transformed. Contact with anything solid caused the fluffy puffs to turn into ravenous space bugs. They ate metal and stone and trees and flowers. An entire city bus was reduced to its tires in seconds.

Metropolis Park became a buffet for the bizarre creatures. There wasn't much they wouldn't or couldn't eat.

Except Superman.

Superman's invulnerable Kryptonian skin was too much for the ravenous bugs. Once their insectoid brains realized that he was not a meal, the creatures departed and went in search of something tastier: Metropolis Bridge!

SNAP! SNAP!

CRUNCH!

The bridge's steel cables were like spaghetti to the alien insects. The cars on the bridge were like meatballs. As the drivers and passengers escaped on foot, Superman flew to the rescue.

The Man of Steel scooped up thousands of the space bugs with his cape and filled it like a giant bag. The fabric of his cape was as indestructible as his skin, so the bugs could not chew through it. Superman crumpled the bulging cape with his super-strength. The bugs were crushed into metal crumbs.

Just then, he heard terrified cries coming from the Daily Planet Building!

The Man of Steel returned to Metropolis. Lois Lane was the first to greet him.

"Superman! You saved Metropolis — again! How about giving me an exclusive interview?" Lois asked.

"I usually only give my interviews to Clark Kent, but okay," Superman said. He smiled, amused by the secret fact that he was actually Clark Kent.

"So what do you think those things were, Superman?" Lois asked. "Aliens? Robots? Robot aliens?"

Superman rubbed his chin. "To be honest, Lois, I'm not quite sure," he said. "Your guess would be as good as mine."

Lois narrowed her eyes. "Well, they're obviously not from this planet, though. Right?" she asked.

"I wouldn't say that," Superman said. "Certain . . . citizens of Metropolis have been known to create robots like these."

Lois's eyes went wide. "Are you implying that Lex Luthor is behind all these pesky robots?" she asked.

Superman smiled. "I have no reason to suspect Lex," he said. "*Yet.*"

Superman had long ago learned to be careful with what he said to reporters. He could trust Lois Lane, though. She had proven that on many different occasions.

While Superman spoke to Lois, he was also checking the skies with his super-vision. He wanted to be absolutely certain there were no more threats to Earth.

* * *

Brainiac sat in his spaceship on the surface of the alien vessel. Methodically, carefully, he assessed the threat he was now facing. A powerful force field held his skull-ship hostage. He was trapped like a specimen in a bottle. Like a rat in a cage.

"If I am to escape, I must know more about what holds me," Brainiac decided.

FWIRRRRSH!
FWIRRRRSH!

Data tendrils snaked out from the skull-ship. They extended down, down, down through the outer layers of the alien vessel.

Sensor pods on each tendril searched for information. One of the sensors finally touched a surface that was not rock or space debris.

"Contact," Brainiac said. "Analyze."

Information flowed into the network of Brainiac's Twelfth-Level Intellect.

ZWOOOOOM!

But something else came with it. Another mind suddenly filled Brainiac's consciousness. It was a sentient mind that was more expansive than anything Brainiac had ever encountered. It invaded his data banks.

The ship sucked up information like a thirsty beast.

"No! Not my data!" Brainiac shouted. "Get out of my memory banks!"

But Brainiac had no defense. The alien intelligence was far more powerful than Brainiac. It took what Brainiac had collected from innumerable worlds and made it its own. Before the data was gone, Brainiac calculated that there was only one possibility of escape.

If he had been human, Brainiac would have called this small chance *hope*.

Through his connection with the alien intelligence, Brainiac showed it an image of Metropolis on Earth.

With all the intensity and power his circuits could muster, Brainiac gave the ship a suggestion. "Go. Collect that city," he ordered. "Add it to your collection."

WOOOOOOOSH!

The gigantic alien vessel started to move. The ship left the orbit of the dying world, heading toward its new destination.

A sinister grin crossed the android's faceplate. "Superman will defend his city," Brainiac said. "He will destroy this alien ship. And when he does, I will be free."

CHAPTER 2

ALIEN ABDUCTION

Clark Kent stood and watched a squad of soldiers battle an onslaught of alien invaders.

ZAP! ZAP!

ZIRRT!

ZIRRRRRRRRT!

Energy weapons blasted from both sides. The humans were outnumbered, but they fought bravely for their survival.

"It would be so easy for Superman to wipe out those bad guys," said a man standing next to Clark.

"Yes, but then the movie would be over in ten seconds," another reporter said.

"Cut!" the director shouted. The human and alien combatants stopped fighting. The man turned to the group of reporters. "Thanks for coming to my preview of *Earth Doom!*"

Clark was covering the event for the Daily Planet. He was an award-winning journalist, but sometimes he liked to take simple assignments like this one.

"The alien makeup is very convincing," Clark commented. "Do you happen to know who designed it?"

As the director answered Clark's question, another reporter pointed to the sky. "Is . . . is that a special effect, too?" he asked.

Everyone looked up at the sky. An enormous, rocky sphere dominated the view.

That's no special effect, Clark thought.

Clark used his telescopic vision for a closer look. What he saw made him spring into action.

This is a job for Superman! he realized.

While everyone was fixated on the looming space rock, Clark Kent slipped away.

SWOOOOOOOOOOSH!

Faster than the speed of sight, Clark removed his business suit, revealing a different sort of suit: his Superman costume!

WOOOOOOOOOOOSH!

He flew at top speed toward the approaching menace.

"Look! There goes Superman!" a reporter declared. "That thing won't last ten seconds against him."

Another reported nodded. "For sure."

"Unexpected," Brainiac observed. "Superman did not attack the alien ship."

Brainiac had anticipated that Superman would destroy the giant vessel, or at least severely damage it, in order to save his precious Metropolis.

"The result of this action is not acceptable. I must recalculate," Brainiac said.

WHIRRRR!

Thousands of possibilities raced through Brainiac's mind like a computer playing a hundred games of chess all at once. He analyzed action and reaction, stimulus and response, over and over again. Brainiac searched for a way to force Superman's hand. He had to find a way to make the Man of Steel take drastic and immediate action.

"I must increase the danger level to Metropolis," Brainiac concluded. "The increased threat of destruction should produce the desired results."

Data tendrils snaked out from his skull-shaped ship. Brainiac explored the memory banks of the alien vessel. He was very careful to avoid the attention of the robotic brain that had almost overwhelmed him earlier. No matter what, Brainiac did not want to be absorbed into its data banks.

Brainiac searched inactive files and low-level information sources. There were countless terabytes of information available, but there was nothing Brainiac considered useful. However, he learned that the alien intelligence had been gathering data for a long time . . .

Brainiac began to experience something similar to an emotion. A human might call it *frustration*. If he could not escape, Brainiac was doomed to become just another scrap of space debris attached to the exterior of the ancient alien spaceship. His Twelfth-Level Intellect rejected that fate. His sense of self-preservation and self-importance made him refuse to admit defeat. So he continued to covertly dig in the archives of the strange ship.

Brainiac prowled through the memory banks of the alien mind like a thief in the shadows. He was impressed with the amount of information stored in the smallest, low-priority files. But finally he found what he needed to spur Superman into action.

"Missiles," Brainiac said. His data tendrils reached into the command system of an ancient defense grid. He set the target coordinates for Metropolis.

"Fire."

* * *

Superman stood atop the Daily Planet Building and looked up at the stars sparkling above. It was just like any other beautiful night in Metropolis — except the brilliant blue globe of planet Earth was overhead!

"I need some perspective," the Man of Steel declared.

Superman flew above Metropolis. He used his super-vision to make sure the people were safe. He did not see anyone in any real danger.

There were traffic jams and mass confusion. The highways leaving the city were cut off. The half-eaten Metropolis Bridge ended in the middle of its span. But the people of the city were unharmed. Metropolis had been lifted from its foundations and put into a cocoon.

"Let's find out who, or what, is behind this," Superman said.

The Man of Steel focused his X-ray vision below the surface of the city. It penetrated the layers of soil and sewers and subways. Then his super-vision encountered the hard rock of the asteroid. Chunks and boulders of space-frozen lead stopped his X-ray vision. He could not see through those portions.

Superman was about to turn his super-vision to another part of the city when a sudden explosion alerted his super-hearing.

KA-BOOOOOM!

He heard the cries of people in danger. One of those voices was from Lois Lane!

Superman lay flat on the ground. The breath was knocked out of his lungs, and his head was spinning. The green dust floating down and covering his body drained the strength from the Man of Steel.

Only one substance could have that effect on the Man of Steel.

"Superman! Are you all right?" Lois Lane asked. She tried to help him up.

"Kryptonite dust," Superman said weakly. "Need to . . . get it off me."

Lois realized Superman's situation immediately. She gestured at the crowd that had gathered around the fallen Man of Steel.

"Come on, everyone. Help me get Superman over to that fire hydrant. We can wash off the Kryptonite dust!" Lois shouted.

Water was gushing out of a broken fire hydrant like a fountain. The crowd lifted the Man of Steel and carefully carried him so his body was underneath the spray. They were all eager to help their hero.

Superman recovered as soon as the green dust rinsed away and flowed down a sewer drain. He thanked his rescuers and flew up into the sky. Those missiles had come from below Metropolis, from somewhere deeper within the asteroid ship. Superman flew through the hole the missiles had made.

Superman gritted his teeth. "I need to know where those weapons came from," he said.

CHAPTER 3

BURIED SECRETS

WOOOOOOOOOOOSH!

Superman sped down the tunnel made by the missiles. It led deep into the rocky layers of the asteroid-like ship.

"How strange — there's an atmosphere down here," the Man of Steel said.

The tunnel opened into what he thought was an enormous cave. A moment later, Superman realized it wasn't a cave at all. "It's a dome of rock and space debris," he said with a gasp. "And there is a city under the dome!"

The Man of Steel was very curious about the city, but he was more concerned about the origin of the missiles. He didn't want to allow more to be fired. So he followed the path deeper and deeper.

Superman's eyes widened as he flew into a new habitat buried below the first one. "Another city!" he said. "What kind of asteroid is this?"

The Man of Steel glimpsed alien architecture and vehicles as he flew. He headed down from the hole in the ceiling toward the hole in the ground. There, he saw insectoid citizens gathered around the opening where the missiles had been launched.

CHITTER! CHITTER!

They made nervous sounds and jumped back in alarm as Superman zoomed past them and down the hole.

"Sorry to startle you!" Superman apologized, even though he knew they couldn't understand him. He continued deeper into the asteroid ship.

The Man of Steel groaned. "There must be more Kryptonite nearby," he said.

Superman used his X-ray vision to scout ahead. His super-vision revealed a startling surprise.

"Another habitat," Superman said. "And it's from Krypton!"

Superman scanned the city buried below him at the end of the tunnel. He recognized the architecture and the clothing. They were from a bygone era in Krypton's history.

The people also looked a lot like him. The buildings were ancient and had been repaired over and over again. There were no vehicles. Funny-looking solar panels sprouted from most of the buildings. The citizens walked along streets that were overgrown with massive trees and other plant life. It was clear that the vegetation had been there a long, long time.

"The deeper into the ship I travel, the older each civilization is," Superman said. "This colony is over a thousand years . . . and its people are my ancestors!"

Superman's super-vision revealed why he was feeling so weak: a glowing red sphere hovered above the city.

"The habitat has a red sun," Superman realized. "It maintains a Kryptonian environment, which means I have no superpowers under its rays."

The Man of Steel could not enter the Kryptonian habitat. He had discovered a living part of his destroyed home world, but he could not set foot on its soil or he would lose his superpowers.

The missiles had come from the Kryptonian colony. When the weapons exploded outside the red-sun environment, they formed puffs of Kryptonite dust.

But it was obvious that the inhabitants had not fired the missiles. Their level of technology had vanished over the many centuries.

So if these people didn't launch the missiles, Superman thought, *then who did?*

Superman flew up the missile tunnel, away from the buried Kryptonian city. It made him sad to leave. It would have been wonderful to meet people who shared a common ancestry with him, especially considering he knew very little about his home planet, Krypton.

Superman knew that entering their habitat would have stripped away his superpowers, but that fact didn't make him feel any better about leaving. Ultimately, he would need those abilities to save Metropolis. And so he sacrificed his only chance at visiting a piece of his former home in order to rescue his current one.

"Well, the mystery of where the missiles came from is solved," Superman said as he flew back up the tunnel. "But I still don't know who fired them, or why."

RUMMMMBLE!

The Man of Steel collapsed the walls as he passed, filling in the tunnel.

PAT! PAT! THUD!

Using the nearby debris, Superman repaired the gaping holes in the ground in each habitat, as well.

ZRRT!

ZRRT!

ZRRT!

He sealed the openings in the rock domes with his heat vision. All of the ancient cities were safe now.

* * *

Metropolis was calm when Superman finally returned. It seemed like any other night in a great metropolitan city.

BEEP BEEP HONK!

Traffic was busy as ever, but the citizens were mostly peaceful. They walked the streets, doing their shopping and playing in the parks.

But Superman knew that things were not normal. Although the citizens couldn't see it, Planet Earth was in the sky, high above the city, instead of the moon!

SZZZZZZT!

Suddenly something sizzled beneath Superman's feet. A bright, hot spot melted the pavement.

WOOOOOSH!

The Man of Steel inhaled, preparing to use his freezing super-breath.

ZRRRT! WIRRRRRT!

Suddenly, Superman saw a small, metallic sphere emerge from the molten hole that formed in the ground. He slowly released his breath, giving the entity a chance to explain itself — whatever it was.

"What is going on here?" Superman said. "Who — or what — are you?"

The sphere floated up to meet Superman's eyes. "Kryptonian," it said. "I require your assistance."

The Man of Steel could hardly believe his ears. Now he knew who was behind the current danger to Metropolis.

"Brainiac!" Superman said. "Are you responsible for all of this?!"

"I do not deny my involvement," Brainiac said flatly.

"Why? What's your scheme this time?" Superman asked.

"As I said, I require your assistance," Brainiac said.

FZZT! CRACKLE!

The orb crackled and glowed with an alien energy.

"And so you take all of Metropolis hostage?" Superman said. "That's an extreme — and dangerous — way to get my attention."

"I had no intention of attracting your notice, but all other options have failed," Brainiac said. "I am trapped on this asteroid ship, just like Metropolis is now. Destroy this vessel, and you will free us both. If you do not destroy it, we are both stuck here. For eternity."

Superman smirked. "So, the spider is caught in another spider's web," he said.

"That is an interesting analogy. I've never been compared to an arachnid before," Brainiac said. "We will have to discuss the merits of that comparison later. But the fact remains: I am trapped here along with your home."

The orb inched closer to Superman's face. "So, Kryptonian, will you assist me in this task or not?"

"If it means I can free Metropolis, yes, I'll help you," Superman said.

The orb blinked. "Good," Brainiac said. "The easiest way to destroy this ship is to —"

"I will not destroy this ship," Superman interrupted. "There are sentient beings on board."

"Then your sentimental attachments will trap us here forever," Brainiac said.

"I will find a way," Superman said.

"I calculate your odds of success to be quite small," Brainiac said.

"That's a chance I'll have to take," Superman said.

CHAPTER 4

UNEASY ALLIES

Superman looked up. A glowing yellow sphere started to form above Metropolis. A substitute sun was beginning to grow.

Superman realized that once the Earth-like environment was complete, Metropolis would become just like the other colonies on the alien ship. It would be trapped forever, gradually buried under layers of rock and space debris. He needed to free the city, and fast.

"I need to find the control center of this ship," Superman said.

"I have access to diagrams of the vessel's layout," Brainiac said. The drone projected a holographic image of the asteroid ship.

ZRRRT!

Superman used his super-vision to examine the vessel. "The core of the actual vessel isn't very large, but the layers of accumulated debris are extremely thick," Superman observed. "This thing has been out here for at least twenty thousand years."

"Your estimate is reasonable," Brainiac said in agreement.

"It will take a while to tunnel down to the control core, even using my heat vision," Superman said. "How powerful is the cutting beam on this drone of yours?"

The Man of Steel did not wait for an answer.

ZAP!

ZAP!

ZAP!

Superman directed bursts of his heat vision at the ground.

CRRRRRUMMMMBLE!

RRRRRRUMMMMBLE!

Street pavement melted and shattered. Superman then began to dig with his hands and fists, burrowing through a spot in the city's foundation and into the asteroid.

"Come on, drone, give me a hand," Superman said.

The Man of Steel disappeared below the surface.

FZZZZT! CRACK-ACKLE!

The drone fired its cutting beams and followed.

The pair drilled their way down through the deep layers of the asteroid ship. Superman switched between his heat vision and his X-ray vision so he could avoid tunneling through any habitats.

KIRRRRRRRSH!

The drone continued to bore with its cutting beam alongside the Man of Steel. All the while, Brainiac monitored their progress from his skull-ship.

A short while later, Superman's heat vision encountered metal instead of stone.

"I've reached the hull of the ship," the Man of Steel said.

TSSSSSSSSSS!

He melted a small hole and grabbed the molten edges with his invulnerable hands.

SHREEEEEE!

Superman used his super-strength to rip open the vessel's metal hull like a cardboard box.

Inside, it was like a huge, hollow ball.

Superman estimated that the ball's diameter was as wide as ten football stadiums. Floating at the center was a shiny metal sphere.

The Man of Steel used his X-ray vision to examine the alien globe. Brainiac used the drone's sensors to scan it, too.

ZWOOM!

A spiral beam of energy struck Superman in the chest. The force almost knocked the Man of Steel back out of the opening in the hull.

ZWOOM!

A second blast instantly destroyed Brainiac's drone.

"I must have activated an automatic defense system," Superman said. "If not, I've just made a bad first impression on whoever is controlling this ship."

* * *

Back on the skull-ship, Brainiac sat at the control panel. The drone's monitoring system had gone completely blank. The last bytes of information from the sensor sweep showed a sudden surge of energy.

"I must find another method of monitoring Superman's actions," Brainiac said.

He still did not want to risk attracting the attention of the alien being, so he searched minor, relatively unimportant data nodes.

An information trail led Brainiac to a weapons activation system. There, he saw the alien ship deploy defensive weapons against its intruder, the Man of Steel.

"Interesting. The defense array is drawing a large percentage of the alien's focus away from other priorities," Brainiac observed. "Superman is finally engaging its attention as I had planned."

Brainiac studied the holographic diagram of the vessel's layout. He tracked command paths and data streams.

"While Superman distracts the ship's mind, I can enter its command nodes and deactivate the force field that holds me," Brainiac determined. "I can escape."

Brainiac sent the electronic order for the force field to disappear from around his ship. He waited. And waited.

"No result," Brainiac observed after a few minutes. "That is unacceptable."

Brainiac was determined to escape the alien vessel at all costs, and that included the destruction of the ship and everything on board. It would be unfortunate to lose the data and information the ship's mind had collected over the centuries. However, survival was Brainiac's first priority.

Brainiac sent a command pulse to the weapons array, launching the entire alien arsenal at the Man of Steel. "An all-out assault will incite Superman to take extreme measures," Brainiac calculated. "He will do what I command — one way or another."

"It's stealing my memories!" Superman said.

The Man of Steel began to see his life pass before his mind's eye. His memories went all the way back to the haziest moment he'd left Krypton. As a baby, he saw his father's face lean over him. He felt his mother gently tuck a blanket around him.

WOOOOOOOSH!

Then there was nothing but a roaring sound and movement.

The Man of Steel twisted inside the blob-like alien's trap in an attempt to escape. That's when he saw the disaster unfolding far below him.

"The robot I defeated a minute ago crashed and ripped open a habitat on the other side of the hull!" Superman realized. "I have to save those people!"

As soon as he said the words, the gooey trap dissolved. He did not know why, but there wasn't any time to care at the moment.

Superman's only concern was saving lives. He flew at super-speed to the rescue!

CHAPTER 5

A MEETING OF THE MINDS

ZOOOOM!

The Man of Steel raced at top speed toward the disaster inside the alien ship. One of the most ancient habitats in the universe was in danger of being destroyed. It was built on the first layer of the alien ship's outer hull, and now the hull was ripped open. Parts of the city and its inhabitants were falling into the hollow core of the ancient alien vessel.

SWOOOOOOOSH!

Superman swooped at super-speed. He snatched up as many citizens as he could out of the air and flew them to safety. At the same time, he carefully blew out puffs of his super-breath.

POOOF! POOF!

The breaths gently pushed people back up through the hole to their habitat.

A few moments later, everyone was returned and safe. But the job wasn't done just yet.

FZZZZZZZZT!
ZRRRRRRRT!

Superman sealed the opening with his heat vision. They would be safe inside their home now.

CRACKLE-FZZZZZT!

A ball of energy flew toward Superman. "Uh-oh," Superman said. "Here comes more trouble."

Superman braced himself for a battle with the newly arrived menace. But the object did not attack him. Instead, it stopped and hovered a few feet away from the Man of Steel.

KIRSSSH-ZRRRT-WIRRRSH!

"Greetings, Kryptonian," said the energy sphere. It sounded more like garbled electronic feedback than a voice.

Superman raised an eyebrow. "Um . . . hello," he said.

"You saved the people of the planet Zonos from harm," the orb said.

Superman nodded. "They were in danger," he said.

"Your behavior is uncommon," the sphere continued. "You are a unique specimen."

"Thanks, I guess," Superman said. "Who are you?"

"I will show you. Please follow this entity," the crackling energy ball instructed.

The orb headed toward the central sphere. "How can I refuse such a friendly invitation?" Superman said.

The orb took its time moving toward its objective, but Superman didn't mind one bit. He didn't ask it to speed up, he just walked behind it patiently. While he had no reason to question who or what the sphere was, he couldn't trust it yet, either. So he made sure to scan as much of the area as possible as they moved.

When they reached the central sphere, a large hatch opened on its surface. The orb dissolved. Its mission was complete.

The moment Superman entered the doorway, a brilliant flash of light illuminated his surroundings.

"Does this Kryptonian interface image comfort you?" the image asked. "There was sadness in your memories."

"You saw my past with that organic blob," Superman said. "Krypton is gone."

"Krypton is not gone," the image said. "The city of Cythonnia still lives."

"Cythonnia is a myth," Superman said. Then a realization hit him. "Unless . . . the colony I saw on this ship is Cythonnia!"

"As long as Cythonnia lives, so does the heritage of Krypton," the image said. "That is my mission, for I am a collector. I preserve samples of dying worlds."

"But Metropolis isn't part of a dying world," Superman told the glowing figure. "Why did you take it?"

The alien sentience did not have a quick answer to the Man of Steel's question. It seemed uncertain. It hesitated. Terabytes of information flowed through its data pathways as it accessed volumes of information.

"I . . . ," the image said. "I cannot remember why I took Metropolis."

* * *

"Success," Brainiac said. "The alien mind is distracted by a simple query from the Kryptonian. Unexpected."

He did not want to admit that he was surprised. Brainiac considered himself the superior intellect in all things. But all the same, he took immediate advantage of the opportunity.

Brainiac accessed the alien ship's force field array. He did not try to hide his activity this time since the alien sentience wasn't watching. It was dealing with Superman's question. Brainiac located the commands that held the skull-ship and turned them off. The shimmering canopy above his spaceship disappeared.

"Engine systems on," Brainiac commanded. His ship roared to life. "Launch."

The skull-shaped spacecraft lifted up and away from the surface of the alien vessel.

Brainiac did not look behind him. Everything he had done was logical. He had escaped. He had survived.

"Our alliance is concluded, Kryptonian," Brainiac said, even though he knew Superman could not hear him.

* * *

"Our alliance is concluded, Kryptonian." Superman heard the voice of Brainiac echo inside the command sphere of the alien ship.

The large image of Kryptonian Superman broke apart.

ZAP!

CRACKLE!

Red sparks of violent energy gathered like a storm in front of the Man of Steel.

"My systems have been infiltrated by an outside mind," the intelligence said. "It calls itself Brainiac . . . and it claims that you are its ally!"

The red sparks grew into lightning. Giant red bolts of energy lashed out at the Man of Steel.

"No!" Superman protested.

KRAKOOOM!

Powerful energy bolts blasted the inside of the command sphere. Superman was forced to dodge them at super speed.

"Brainiac tricked us both!" Superman declared between dodges. "Search my memory about him, and you will learn the truth!"

A tendril of blue light struck the Man of Steel in the forehead. He felt his memories flow out of him and into the alien sentience. Every encounter with Brainiac streamed though his mind. It was very unpleasant.

FWAZIRRT!

Finally, the alien intelligence released him."This Brainiac is a unique specimen," the intelligence stated. "It requires more study."

There was a quick flash of light from a teleportation beam. Suddenly Brainiac appeared next to Superman.

"I should have known you'd betray me," Superman told Brainiac.

"Then you should not have agreed to our alliance," Brainiac said flatly.

"Kryptonian, I will return Metropolis to its planet. You may depart with it," the alien sentience proclaimed. "The Brainiac intelligence will remain."

"Unacceptable," Brainiac said.

"Appropriate," Superman said. "Besides, both of you are collectors. I'm sure you'll have plenty to talk about — for a long, long time to come."

The Man of Steel said goodbye to the alien sentience and flew back up the tunnel to Metropolis. As soon as Superman arrived, the city began to lift away from the surface of the asteroid ship. The artificial sun started to dim. The great blue globe of Earth loomed overhead.

Superman flew to the upper reaches of Earth's atmosphere and watched the asteroid-shaped ship leave Earth's orbit.

Hovering in the air high above Metropolis, Superman searched with his super-vision to find anyone hurt by the city's landing back on Earth.

"Brainiac brought a major menace to Earth to save himself," Superman said as he looked over Metropolis. "I hope that's the last cosmic menace I have to face. At least for a little while."

REE-OOOOOO!

REE-OOOOOO!

Suddenly Superman's super-hearing caught the wail of police sirens and fire trucks. He aimed his super-vision down at Earth and scanned the surface for anything suspicious.

A moment later, Superman spotted smoke rising from a section of the city. It had been damaged from landing back on the planet.

WOOOOOOOOOOOSH!

The Man of Steel leaped into the sky and flew to the rescue at super-speed.

"Back to normal!" Superman said.

BIOGRAPHIES

Laurie Sutton has read comics ever since she was a kid. She grew up to become an editor for Marvel, DC Comics, Starblaze, and Tekno Comix. She has written Adam Strange for DC Comics, Star Trek: Voyager for Marvel, plus Star Trek: Deep Space Nine and Witch Hunter for Malibu Comics. There are long boxes of comics in her closet where there should be clothing and shoes. Laurie has lived all over the world and currently resides in Florida.

Luciano Vecchio was born in 1982 and currently lives in Buenos Aires, Argentina. With experience in illustration, animation, and comics, his works have been published in the US, Spain, the UK, France, and Argentina. His credits include Ben 10 (DC Comics), Cruel Thing (Norma), Unseen Tribe (Zuda Comics), and Sentinels (Drumfish Productions).

SKETCHES

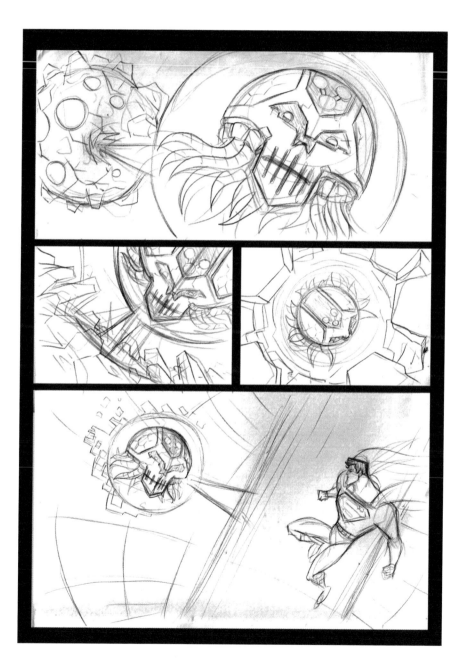

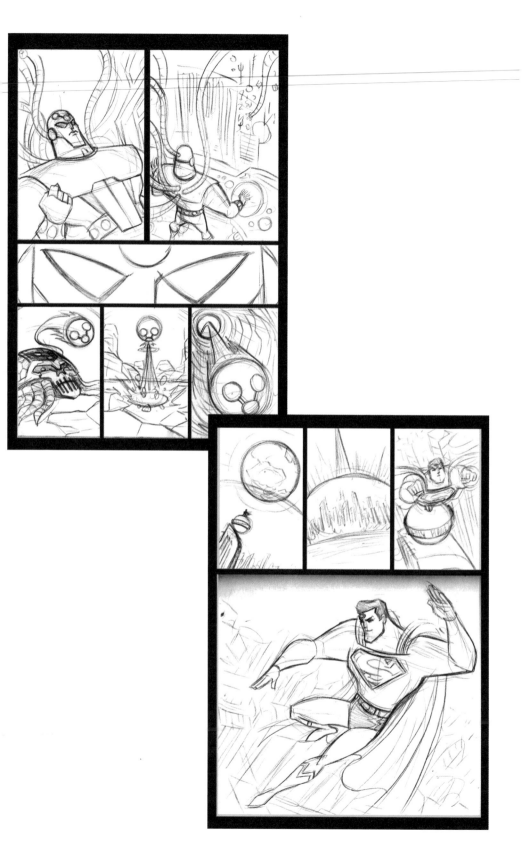

FINAL ART

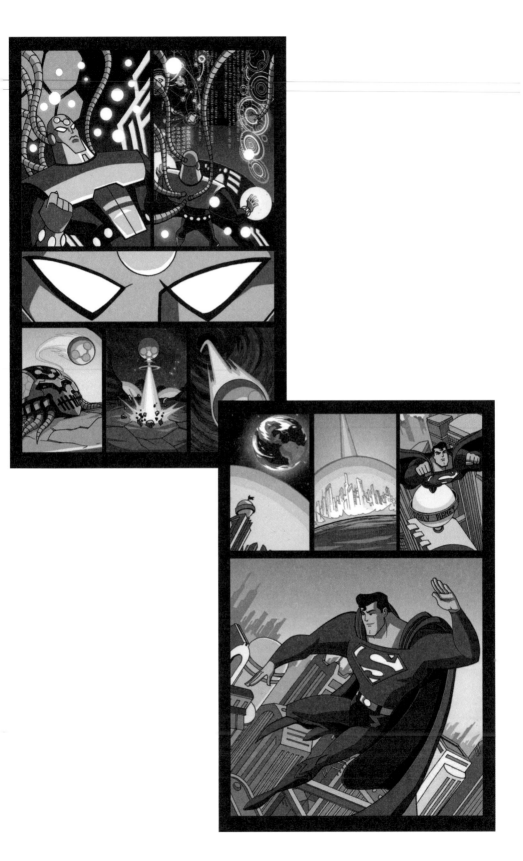

COMICS TERMS

caption (KAP-shuhn)—words that appear in a box. Captions are often used to set the scene.

gutter (GUHT-er)—the space between panels or pages

motion lines (MOH-shuhn LINES)—illustrator-created marks that help show motion in art

panel (PAN-uhl)—a single drawing that has borders around it. Each panel is a separate scene on a spread.

SFX (ESS-EFF-EKS)—short for sound effects. Sound effects are words used to show sounds that occur in the art of a comic.

splash (SPLASH)—a large illustration that often covers a full page (or more)

spread (SPRED)—two side-by-side pages in a comic book

word balloon (WURD BUH-loon)—a speech indicator that includes a character's dialogue or thoughts. A word balloon's tail leads to the speaking character's mouth.

GLOSSARY

analyze (AN-uh-lize)—to study something closely and carefully to learn its nature

ancestry (AN-sess-tree)—a person's ancestors, or the people who were in their family in past times

atmosphere (AT-muhss-feer)—the mass of gases that surrounds a planet or star

cosmic (KOZ-mik)—of or relating to the universe, outer space, or very large or important things

deny (di-NYE)—to say that something is not true, or to refuse something or someone

drastic (DRASS-tik)—severe, serious, or extreme

drone (DROHN)—an unmanned aircraft, ship, or device

harvest (HARR-visst)—gather

perish (PARE-ish)—to die or end

sentimental (senn-tuh-MEN-tuhl)—appealing to the emotions, especially in an excessive way

VISUAL QUESTIONS

1. Brainiac's ship is skull-shaped and has a weird symbol on its forehead. Where else does this symbol show up in this book?

2. This three-panel sequence shows a drone that Brainiac released from the ship. Where is the drone going? What is its goal?

3. In this panel we see three circular images. What do they represent? Why was this done?

4. Here we see Superman destroying some space bugs using his super-speed and a volcano. What other powers could he have used to stop these galactic pests?

5. Lines in the background of this panel extend outward from the explosion. Why was this done? How does it make you feel?